Father wakes the kids,

Charlie gets dressed,

Hilary feeds herself,

Father takes the bus,

and the yawn goes on.

Mother works in the office,

Charlie goes to school,

Hilary plays at day-care,

and the yawn goes on.

After school it's off to the park,

home on the bus,

then Father gives the baths,